This book belongs to

....

B
a

A Red Fox Book

Published by Random House Children's Books
61-63 Uxbridge Road, London W5 5SA,

A RANDOM HOUSE GROUP COMPANY
London Melbourne Sydney Auckland
Johannesburg and agencies throughout the world

25 27 29 31 30 28 26

First published in Great Britain by Andersen Press Ltd 1981
Red Fox edition 1992

Addresses for companies within The Random House Group Limited can
be found at :www.randomhouse.co.uk/offices.htm

Printed in China

THE RANDOM HOUSE GROUP Limited Reg. No. 954009
www.rbooks.co.uk

ISBN 978 0 099 87400 3

A
DARK, DARK
TALE

For William, Edward and Alice Cowling

A
DARK, DARK
TALE

Ruth Brown

RED FOX

Once upon a time there
was a dark, dark moor.

**On the moor there was
a dark, dark wood.**

**In the wood there was
a dark, dark house.**

At the front of the house
there was a dark, dark door.

Behind the door there
was a dark, dark hall.

In the hall there were
some dark, dark stairs.

Up the stairs there was
a dark, dark passage.

Across the passage was
a dark, dark curtain.

Behind the curtain was
a dark, dark room.

In the room was a dark, dark cupboard.

In the cupboard was
a dark, dark corner.

In the corner was
a dark, dark box.

And in the box there
was . . . A MOUSE!

Other Red Fox picture books
from Ruth Brown